Shakespeare Makes the Playoffs

Shakespeare Makes the Playoffs

RON KOERTGE

CANDLEWICK PRESS

Copyright © 2010 by Ron Koertge

First edition 2010

Library of Congress Cataloging-in-Publication Data

Koertge, Ronald.
Shakespeare makes the playoffs / Ron Koertge. — 1st ed.
p.   cm.
Summary: Fourteen-year-old Kevin Boland, poet and first baseman, is torn between his cute girlfriend Mira and Amy, who is funny, plays Chopin on the piano, and is also a poet.
ISBN 978-0-7636-4435-2
[1. Novels in verse. 2. Poetry—Fiction. 3. Interpersonal relations—Fiction. 4. Baseball—Fiction.]   I. Title.
PZ7.5K66Sh 2010
[Fic]—dc22   2009014519

09 10 11 12 13 14 MVP 10 9 8 7 6 5 4 3 2 1

Printed in York, PA, U.S.A.

This book was typeset in Cheltenham.

Candlewick Press
99 Dover Street
Somerville, Massachusetts 02144

visit us at www.candlewick.com

To all the readers of *Shakespeare Bats Cleanup*
who wanted to know what happened next

Look What I Bought You!

I come in tired
from baseball practice, and Dad catches me
guzzling OJ right out of the carton.

"Want a journal?" he asks. "You're a writer.
All writers need journals."

I put the orange juice away and hold out my mitt,
the one Mom bought me. "I'm a first baseman."

"Who used to write poetry. Your teammates
called you Shakespeare." He hands me a notebook.
"And it doesn't have to be poetry. It doesn't
even have to be a journal. It could be a diary."

He lays it on the table, opens to the first page, and writes
with his favorite gel pen: *Shakespeare's*
Secret
Diary

Maybe I should start again. I play ball a lot, because if I
don't, I get rusty.

All I need now are some secrets.

Non-Secret #1

The batting cages are on Bellefontaine.
Dad takes the twisty-turny frontage road.
That way we get to see the backs of things:
a bunch of crows line up like bitter verbs,
some tattooed guys check out a custom ride,
two kids with flashlights practice being spies.

Once there, Dad's cell lights up and plays a tune.
The first few bars, at least. He turns away.
"Yeah, hi. Of course. I'll call you in a sec."
I take my bat and use the resin bag.
Dad gives the guy who runs this place a ten.

A practice swing or two, and then I'm good.
I set the speed for thirty/thirty-five.
I want a baffling, sharply breaking curve.
I want a knuckler with a wicked drop.
I want to hit the sweet spot every time
and bring the roaring crowd right to its feet.

I look around. All guys, all serious,
all twice as old as me. Except one girl.
She's maybe nine, with diamonds in both ears.
Her dad adjusts her goofy stance. Mine talks
to someone I don't know. He starts to grin.

I up the speed to forty-five. I try
to burn holes in the net with red-hot drives.
At last I get deep in the zone. It's great!
And then it's gone. I miss three in a row,
then chop a fastball down the first-base line.
The guy a cage away gives up some props:
"You got a bread-and-butter swing, my man."
"I'm not so sure. Those last ones weren't so hot."
"Trust me: if you can run, you got the tools."
I find my dad, who says, "You looked real good
this time." He musses up my hair. He turns
my hat around. He walks me to the car.

Duty Calls

At home, I have to call Mira.
Do I want to? Sort of.
Do I have to? Absolutely.

First, I find my thesaurus
and look up a couple of words:
preference and *necessity.*

I love my thesaurus. I like
to think about all the words
in there, cuddling up together
or arguing. Montagues on
one side, Capulets on the other.
Synonyms and antonyms.

Dad was right. Writing is fun.
There's nobody besides
this diary I can talk to
like this.

Not the guys I play ball
with and for sure

not Mira.

The Only Child

In their living room, Mira's
parents have these paintings:
Mira looking gorgeous,
her mom looking noble,
her dad looking serious.

Then there's this big one
of the whole family.

You know how in most pictures
people look out, like at the camera
or the painter?

In this one, only Mira does that.
The other two look right at her.

They're the bookends.
She's the first edition.

The Actual Call

"What'd you do today?" Mira asks.

"Took some batting practice with Dad."

"I went to dance class. It was hard."

I've got a zombie movie on mute.
I picture those guys in tutus.
A little too much allegro,
and body parts start falling off.

Baseball is more fun than ballet.
(Okay, maybe not more fun than
Swan Lake Zombies.)

"Did you get hits?" she asks.
"At the cage? Yeah. I did."

We listen to each other listen
to each other breathe. I can't
tell her I wrote blank verse
about batting practice.
She thinks blank verse
means a poem about nothing.

Dad's Somewhere

and he wouldn't mind, anyway,
so I go into his studio and borrow
some printer paper.

I like it that's he's "somewhere."
Not a secret exactly; he just doesn't
tell me.

He doesn't nag me, either, about
where I'm going. He knows my friends.
He knows I'm not going to do
anything stupid.

I'm basically a good kid. But imperfect
enough to be interesting.

Like a good poem.

Like Father Like

I don't bother to hide this diary
(which is actually a red spiral
notebook) because Dad's no snoop.

We're kind of like roommates. His
stuff and my stuff. His life and my
life.

Except for our DNA. Ours.
The polymers and nucleotides.
They'd know each other anywhere.

There's this guy I play ball with sometimes,
a center fielder with a bazooka arm, who
hates his dad. Hates him. Takes
the field all hulked out. Cusses
and spits.

Know why? Because his dad cusses
and spits.

My dad reads and writes. Except
for baseball, that's what I do.

My Dad the Sorcerer

I like how he trashes his books.
You'd think a writer wouldn't do that.

Does A-Rod ever leave his Yankee
jersey outdoors, much less his steroids?

Dad's books are everywhere. Like
his favorite pocket dictionary.

In the rain. Then the sun. It's
as wrinkled as an elephant's butt.

And he loves it. Here's the best part:
it's completely out of order.

Pages go any old place: 57 next
to 109. *Z*'s next to *K*'s. *L*'s beside *C*'s.

I ask him, "How can you use that?"
He's serious when he says, "Divination."

I have to look that up—"insight via omens
and supernatural powers."

Poetry 101

The stanzas in "My Dad the Sorcerer" look like couplets,
but they're really just two lines lying down together.

Couplets gallop (iambic pentameter, for the record)
<u>and</u> they rhyme.

> I went downtown and bought a little hat.
> I took it home and put it on my cat.

That's a couplet. And here's the funny thing: perfect
meter and perfect rhymes get boring after a while.
So what's a poet to do?

Mr. Beauclaire, my English teacher, put this on the board
the other day:

> Wounded, the soldier staggered toward the barn.
> His feet were numb, his uniform was torn.

The first line staggers just like the soldier, and *barn/torn*
clash a little because this isn't a pretty scene.

Then he made us go through the poems in our textbook
and look for stuff where the "mistakes" were perfect.

He calls rhyme a benevolent bully because it'll make a poet look hard for just the right word and then maybe he finds an even better one!

There's a guy—Morton Gluck—who plays for OSH and he's a bully. Rides Fabian and me constantly, and there's nothing sweeter than shutting him up with a standing double. Would I concentrate that hard if it wasn't for him?

Morton Gluck. Imagine waking up every morning in a house full of Glucks.

Love at First Bounce

I love my first baseman's mitt.
I sleep with it. Ball in the pocket,
big rubber band around everything.

It took me three months, easy,
to break it in. Just using it. Not
bullying it. Treating it right
with neat's-foot oil.

(*Neat* is a really old word for cows.
So I guess at some time in history,
a foreman said, *Round up them
thar neats, boys, and head 'em
for the Rio Grande.* Or maybe not.)

I've seen guys bake their gloves
or soak them in motor oil.
Know what that does? It ruins
them, that's what.

Mitt as destiny. Seriously.
It's like choosing an instrument
for band. Tuba player is to catcher
as clarinet is to first base. Once
a tuba player, always a tuba player.

I can't take my long, beaky-looking
first baseman's mitt to left field.
Nobody does that.

I tried to explain it all to Mira
once and she said, "What's the
difference? It's just something
to catch the ball with."

She's never going to understand.

Back to the Past

Mom bought the glove for me.
Not for my birthday or a bunch
of A's. Not for anything really.

We just went to Sports Chalet
one night and tried a few on.
Bought the Wilson A2K,
top of the line, as good as it gets.

I told her I was fine with my
old glove.

But she said, "No, I want you
to have something that will last
a long time."

Now I'm pretty sure she knew she
was sick. I'll bet she was afraid
that she didn't have

a long time.

The Bird Man of Middle School

I'm doing math homework for Mr. Vogel:

Jack, who in two years will be twice as old as everybody,
leaves Chicago going a hundred miles an hour on a
unicycle. How long before he reaches Jill?
Show your work.

and I'm so bored, I look up his name in an online
German-English dictionary. Guess what *Vogel* means
in English. Bird.

He's big and bald and a tyrant. And his last name is Bird.
That night I text a couple of classmates and we spend a few
minutes making fun of him—sitting on little blue eggs,
eating worms, getting chased by a cat—

and then we solve the problems which are, all of a sudden,
easier.

Saturday

I'm meeting Mira at the library.
Fabian and I ride over on our bikes.
Jennifer and Becca are there, but not
the tardy Mira. The dilatory Mira.
The loiterer. Mira the Leisurely.

Becca checks us out and grins. She flirts
with everybody. It doesn't mean
anything. Jennifer looks everywhere
but at us. That's just her way.

There are a couple of other girls hanging
around. Maybe only two years older,
but they might as well be from another
galaxy. Big raccoon eyes and red high-tops.
They lie on the grass like castaways.

When Mira hops out of her mom's SUV,
Fabian says, "She is way cute."

He's right. Mustard-colored pants.
Pastrami-pink top.

Wait a minute. Is she really cute, or am I
just hungry?

Cute

All right, secret diary. Do your duty. I'll write fast
so the truth can get out. I know it's in there. If I'm
not careful, I lie to myself. Even in this notebook
nobody'll ever see.

So here we go. At top speed.

Mira is cute. I know that. But I wonder if she's cuter
since Fabian said so. I'm used to her cuteness.
Then Fabian points it out and suddenly she's cuter.
I'm gladder to see her. I'm impressed that Fabian
is impressed. I like it that he likes her. I admire
his admiration. All of a sudden I like Mira more
even though she's the same girl I was kind of fed up
with twelve hours ago.

I know what some guys would say: "Don't sweat it,
man. Girls are like buses. There's another one along
every twenty minutes."

But nobody really wants to take a bus, do they?
Everybody wants
a limo.

On the Shores of Gitche Gumee Middle School

Just across the burning asphalt
at the busy intersection,
restless students by the dozens
mill around and punch each other.
More like ducklings than sixth graders
we all stagger toward the sidewalk.
Older guys are playing roundball
while their girlfriends lie like panthers
on the hoods of pricey Hondas
black and sleek like tricked out spaceships
from a planet with no sun.
By the Coke machine, the Goth kids
sprawl like shadows on the green grass
as the skaters try for big air
off the ramp that says DON'T SKATE HERE.
All around me is the plumage
of the current flock of scholars:
Rick in stylish Abercrombie,
George in shabby thrift-store splendor.
Sean, the phantom of the classroom,
Lil, the brain with all the answers.
Teacher's pet and teacher's nightmare,
one sits ringside, one's a cheater.
Girls in serious procession
cruise the aisles before they settle.

Boys in khaki and in denim
gather by the perfect blackboard,
gather by a handmade map of
the lost continent Atlantis,
water streaming from its towers
made of jade and gold and diamonds.
Coronado and Vespucci,
Magellan and Balboa, all
half-crazed with El Dorado.
"What's up, Shakespeare," says a tall kid
who played second for Pop's Plumbing.
At the bell the teacher rises
in her brand-new shoes and jacket.
"Settle down now. No more talking.
If you're plotting any mischief
expect eons of detention.
You will hear my scornful laughter
as you rot down in the basement."
She means business. Textbooks open.
Some guy fondles his new cell phone.
Eyes drift toward the sun-stunned windows.
May we live in peace together.
May we get along and prosper.

At least till lunch.

Held Hostage by Hiawatha

That last poem was all in Hiawatha rhythm,
this special kind of meter that Henry Wadsworth
Longfellow used.

Today Henry's kind of a relic. And to be fair,
"The Song of Hiawatha" isn't the kind of thing
anybody can read between innings, if you know
what I mean.

But it's full of rushing rivers, a ton
of silent forests, and lovely Minnehaha
in her little buckskin skirt.

Wait! Did you hear that?

For a while it was all my dad and I
could do to carry on a normal conversation:

"How 'bout pancakes for our breakfast
or a bowl of steaming oatmeal?"

Hilarious, but Hiawatha really got into
our cells. It was two days before we could talk
like normal human beings.

Biographical P.S.

Longfellow's first wife, Mary, died young,
so he got married to Fanny Appleton. They had
kids and Fanny wanted to keep some
of her daughters' hair, so she put a few curls
in envelopes and was melting wax to seal them
when her dress caught fire.

Longfellow tried to put out the flames but all
he did was get scars on his hands and face.

Even when he healed, it hurt to shave, so he
grew a beard.

That's just about the saddest thing I ever heard.

After-School Special

I'm riding beside Mira. She's walking, but I've got
her backpack on my handlebars, so she's—here's a cool
word—unencumbered.

I want to tell her about that fire and Longfellow's beard,
but that's kind of a buzz kill. Not that there's much
buzz to kill.

I could show her the poem I wrote about it, but I gave her
one once and she lost it.

She said she was sorry and wanted another copy,
but I said my printer was down. Wonderfully mature,
Kevin. Did you kick the slats out of your crib, too?

My neighborhood is so quiet it's like walking through ruins.
I wonder what she's thinking.

"Kevin, c'mere."

She leads me behind one of the big oaks and puts both arms
around my neck. Mira likes to make out in semipublic.

If her mother only knew.

Talk About a Buzz Kill

I come in the front door hot from making
out with Mira. My synapses are popping.
My blood is sizzling and pulsing. If there
was dark, I'd glow in it.

And there's my dad at the dining-room table,
weeping. Not just crying. Weeping.

After Mom died, somebody from the hospital
gave us her things — a turquoise bracelet,
her cell phone, her clothes in a plastic bag,
her purse with money wadded up in it.

When we got home, Dad sat right at this table,
ironed everything with the edge of his hand,
then put her twenties, her tens, her fives
and ones
all
in
order.

He's doing it again. Opening and closing
her phone, handling the bracelet, smoothing
out the money.

His face is red, what hair he's got is messed up,
his nose is running.

I don't know what to say. Do other guys'
dads cry?

If they do, nobody talks about it.

I Know What Dad's Going Through

Sadness is a big dark bus
with a schedule of its own.
But when it pulls up and the door
opens with a hiss, you pretty much
have to get on.

I usually go to the ball field.
If there's a game, it's perfect:
I think about that. Grief can just
loiter by the water fountain
in his big, stupid shroud.

I like to move. I like to feel
my heart beat. Grief wears big,
ugly shoes and can't keep up.

When there's nobody around,
I just throw into the backstop
until I can't anymore.

I aim right at Grief. I hit
him and I hit him and I hit him
and pretty soon he gives up
like the chicken-shit thing
he is.

Here's What I Did This Time

Dad's downstairs pulling
himself together.
I get out this notebook
and I write a poem. Fast.

So much for "emotion
recollected in tranquility,"
which is what Dad told me
a really old poet named
Wordsworth said poetry was.

I thought about that a little
though and I totally knew
what he meant. Stuff happens.
Serious stuff, intense stuff.
Wounds, okay? Shrapnel.

And later on you sort it out.
Poems need to be put together
right. Some details fit, some
really don't. Poems aren't
grab bags. You know how
people say, "Anything goes"?
Well, not in poetry, it doesn't.

Knock, Knock

Next day, Dad asks, "You're coming to the reading,
right?"

I look up from my desk. "Saturday night? For sure."

"And you're going to sign up for open mike?"

"Uh-huh. I wrote about going to the batting cages.
It's blank verse, but nobody'll know. It's just kind
of a story."

He looks down, then up, then down again. "I might
bring Anna, this woman I met at yoga class. I wasn't
crying the other day just because your mom's gone.
I didn't think I'd ever like anybody again, and now I do.
A little, anyway."

I just nod.

What does he want me to say? Go ahead and forget
Mom so you can like this Anna person?

No way.

Here's That Poem I Wrote Real Fast
the Other Day, the One About Mom's Money

Full of grief my father stands
money filling up his hands.

Money that belonged to them.
Now it's owned by only him.

The ones, the fives, the wrinkled tens
go side by side like sets of twins.

This must help him make some sense,
these solemn green dead presidents.

Not bad except now I need a stanza about
this Anna. Which rhymes with *Havana.*
Which is where I wish she was.

Mira Called Me Tonight

and we talked for about an hour.
I gotta say—I like this part:

the *O*'s in her words are like
little balloons sometimes.

I remember how cute she is,
how she always smells good.

I'm listening and looking
out the window: I've left
half a tangerine on my desk
and it's almost glowing.

Then all of a sudden
the temperature changes
and she's mad about Becca.
Because of her, I mean.

Mira had this plan that
she and Jennifer and Becca
would be friends forever
and nothing would ever
get in the way.

But now for Becca, boys
come first.

Written on the Way to the Reading:
A Mobile Pantoum

I've got a few things on my mind.
We don't have far to go.
There's just enough time to chat.
I'm curious about Anna.

We don't have far to go.
So I ask about Dad's "girlfriend."
I'm curious about Anna:
Is she pretty? Is she nice?

I ask about his "girlfriend."
The one he met in yoga class.
Is she pretty? Is she nice?
What's he going to say—no?

The one he met in yoga class.
It had to happen. He's only forty-two.
What's he going to say—no?
She sounds so different from Mom.

It had to happen. He's only forty-two.
Anna's from Manila. She's a nurse.
She sounds so different from Mom.
I've got a few things on my mind.

The Book Bungalow

I get nervous before I read. It's no big deal.
Just one poem that not everybody listens to,
anyway, and sometimes the applause totally
defines *perfunctory* (imagine the sound
a seal makes if he's got sore flippers)

but it's still something I want to be good at.
If I can stand at the plate while some titanic
sixteen-year-old throws smoke, I can get up
in front of thirty-two people and read a poem.

Almost my favorite part is going to sign up
for the open mike. There's usually a sheet
on the bulletin board or by the cash register.
I already recognize a couple of people.
Regulars on the local poetry circuit:

The guy who looks like Whitman and writes
about his mother. The lady who holds up
a mirror and looks at herself while she reads.
The homeless guy with the dog and the three-
thousand-page poem he keeps in his grocery
cart but won't show anybody. The one who
yells, the one who cusses, the one who cries,
the one who's been abducted. Again.

And then there's me with blank verse about
the batting cages.

Dad leads me toward the cash register.
"I want you to meet Ophelia," he says.
"She owns this joint."

On the way he asks, "Where's Mira?"
"Where's Anna?"
"Anna's working a double shift."
"Mira says she's got too much homework."
"Then it's just you and me and a few friends
from another galaxy."

A Few Words About the Setting

The BB is actually a pretty cool place.
A real bungalow. Nooks and crannies.
Sofas and chairs with soft, beat-up
cushions that look like fat ghosts
are already sitting in them. Wall-to-wall
volumes, (free) tea and Oreos on a table
that's wearing two bunny slippers on
its front feet. Cat with a chewed-up ear
asleep on a dictionary.

I shake hands with Ophelia. Her hair
looks like it can't make up its mind,
her T-shirt says LET THERE BE LIGHT.

"This is Amy." She nods toward a girl
in velvety-looking overalls, which I
immediately like because overalls
are work clothes and velvet is for lying
on a couch and eating little sandwiches.

"But you can call me Trixie," Amy says.
Her mother warns, "Don't start."

Trixie/Amy hands me the clipboard.
"Wanna read?"

I've heard that one a million times:
It's a challenge. A double dare.
You'll never hit this guy, Boland.
He's got your number. And if I happen
to swing and miss: *Nice cut. How*
about a tennis racket next time?

"I already signed up."

It only stops her for a second, but it stops her.
Like a clean single right past the shortstop.

Open Mike

I'm on right after "Making Out in the Closet,"
which was hilarious. I have to wait for people
to stop laughing. But I've been up after the guy
who hit a grand slam, so I put on
my (pretend) poetry helmet and step up.

Dad told me to make sure everybody knew
I was reading blank verse, but almost everybody
here is a writer. They know blank verse
when they hear it. So if they applaud,
they mean it.

Then right after me, Amy/Trixie strolls up,
completely empty-handed, and says, "Grapefruit
Soliloquy." I don't know what the lines looked
like, but here's what she said:

> All that time on the tree, then boxed up, put
> on a truck first and then a plane only to end
> up in a pile with a lot of other large citrus.
>
> Okay, I've been picked, but what I want
> to know is this: when will I be chosen?

She knew it by heart, too. How cool is that?

Let's Give It Up for Daniel Boland

After the break, it's Dad's turn. He's good on his feet.
Easy to like. He's reading from his short story that just
came out in *Tin House,* a magazine that publishes
very cool fiction.

People quiet down when he reads. Not just because
they're polite, either. The story gets a grip on them.

I listen but I also think about making out with Mira.
The whole semipublic thing. Her parents are so strict.
Is she trying to get caught? If that happens, you know
whose fault it'll be: mine. Her dad thinks his precious
little angel daughter would never even hold hands
if some boy wasn't twisting her other arm.

When It's Over

I like being one of the poets. We stand around and say
nice things to each other. They're 24 and 46 and 73
but we're all in this together. I could never play ball
with a 24 yr. old phenom. I'd look like such a kid.
Here I'm just another poet.

The cat that was asleep on the dictionary (His name
is Styx. With a *Y*. Like the river.) comes over
and rubs up against me. Shasta says, "You're lucky.
Styx is a harsh critic. He bit me after a reading once."

Then the place clears out. I'm sitting by myself on
a swaybacked couch and kind of wondering
if a famous butt ever preceded mine when Amy
(I'm not calling her Trixie) plops down next to me.

"You did pretty good. It's not easy to go on after
a really funny poem."
"You did good, too. That batting cage poem
was kind of new, but I've read it over a lot
and there's still no way I could just recite it."
She bites a cookie in half and offers what's left to me.
"I didn't recite it," she says. "I didn't know what
I was going to say until I got up there."
"No way."

"I'm the last one on at every open mike. But I don't plan anything. That's why it's fun."

She's still holding out that cookie, which I kind of want. Maybe if I pant and fetch the newspaper she'll feed it to me.

"You go to Central Middle School?" she asks. "Do you know Mr. Beauclaire?"

"He's my teacher."

"Comes in here all the time. Very cool guy."

"Why aren't you at Central?"

"Because I go to Fair Oaks Arts." She points over her shoulder, then runs her fingers over an invisible keyboard. "I play piano."

People stop and say good-bye to Amy. I'll bet she's fourteen like me but easy around grown-ups. She's sitting kind of cross-legged, and I can see her sandals used to have tread on them but they're smooth now, like dangerous tires.

In Class

I'm watching Mr. Beauclaire write a poem
on the board and looking up synonyms on my laptop.
Beautiful, comely, gorgeous, good-looking,
attractive.

None of them is quite right, and what am I doing
thinking about Amy, anyway? I've got a girlfriend.

I'll think about Mr. B. in the Book Bungalow—
chatting with Ophelia, then settling into one of those
hippo-size couches with a cup of Red Zinger.

He fits there. A lot of teachers don't fit anywhere
but school. I saw my geography teacher, Ms. Baldwin,
in Target once and I thought, *What are you doing*
out of your room? Like she stood in the corner
at night on Sleep Mode and then at 7:30 the principal
came by and switched her to Hyper-Teach.

Mr. Beauclaire deserves a page of his own in this diary.

Mr. B.

climbs mountains every summer. The tattoo
on his forearm is a stick of dynamite with a sizzling fuse.
He never goes anywhere without a book, even Tibet.
Especially, he says, Tibet.

He came home from there once totally sick.
He read Emily Dickinson in the hospital
and the sun on her white dress made him well.
He says.

Emily Dickinson lowered cookies to the neighborhood
kids from a second-story window, making sure they never
saw her face. THEN she sat down and wrote killer poems
on the backs of envelopes.

Emily (he says to call her Emily, to think of her as Emily,
somebody who—let's face it—is extraordinary but is still
just Emily) had a friend named Thomas Wentworth
Higginson who said, "I never was with anyone who drained
my nerve power so much. I am glad not to
live near her."

He knows all kinds of stories like that. He makes poets
into people like the rest of us: people with sinus trouble,
people with a lot of bills, people with car trouble or heart
trouble. All that and they write poetry anyway.

When somebody in the back row asks him, "What does
this poem mean?" he says, "Don't worry so much
about what it means. Pretend poetry is chili
and you're starving. Would you ask what chili means?
Just eat it up."

Better Late than Never

I promised myself I'd brood a little over that
"Mobile Pantoum," the one I wrote on the way
to the reading. The reading where Amy got up
in those velvet overalls and—

Stop that, Kevin. Concentrate.

That pantoum is a pretty good form for what went on
in the car while Dad and I were talking. I ask, he
answers, I think about what he said and go over it
again, he repeats himself.

Sometimes pantoums rhyme; some don't. Rhyme
is like sugar anyway: too much of a good thing
if you're not careful.

Pantoums are a get-used-to-it-gradually form.
Two steps forward, one back. They're never
in a hurry. There's no such thing
as a supersonic pantoum.

I Go Two-for-Four

against the guys from All-Green Cleaners.
Mira doesn't come to the game. Or Dad.

Just a few bored parents.
Plus Morton Gluck and his big mouth.

A fan like that is called the tenth man.
He rides the other team, tries to
throw them off-balance.

But Morton rags on both sides.
Constantly. I've seen moms move
away from him.

He's trouble. I can feel that
coming.

Waiting for Mira after School

She waves from about seventy lockers away, then when she
gets up close before I can say anything, she blurts,

"I can't wear this top anymore. Farmers who grow cotton
use 23 percent of the world's insecticides. And polyester
can be ironed at a lower temperature and that saves energy."

"Let me guess: Earth Science, right?"

"Promise me you won't drink out of plastic bottles,
either. People throw away forty million a day
and they take a thousand years to degrade."

She hands me her books. What am I—the Donkey of Love?

"Saturday we're going to help clean up the L.A. River.
Everybody will be there."

"Really? Everybody? Sounds kind of crowded."

"Will you be serious for a change!"

I nod, but I'm not so sure it's good for a poet to be serious.
I mean there's a lot of that already going around.
Do we really need more?

Dinner with Dad

He likes to cook. He takes good care of me.

But I still miss my mom. For a while
when I set the table I'd put out a plate for her.

There it sat. That was awful. It was like she
was just in the kitchen or the bathroom and any
minute she'd come in and sit down.

But tonight he's made mac and cheese, and while we're
eating, he says, "Anna wants us to come to her place
Saturday night. It doesn't mean anything.
It's no big deal.

"I'm not going to marry her. I'm not going to marry
anybody. I didn't date much when I was young,
so I might want to see what that's like. Go out with
different kinds of gals. You understand, don't you?"

Gals. Different kinds of gals. Oh, my God!

Nightmares About Different Kinds of Gals

She parks her Harley at the curb. Steel-tipped boots,
leather jacket, one gold tooth, tatts everywhere.
"So your name's Kevin. There's got to be room
somewhere on this old bod for a little more ink.
How about right here under BORN TO CRUISE?"

Long skirt and bonnet. Two men with beards carry in
a churn. "My loom and spinning wheel are right outside.
I'll make all your clothes. My homemade pants are mostly
flax. They're the talk of the commune."

One moving van pulls up, then another. A woman
climbs out of a VW followed by kids. And more kids.
All of them with colds. "They're named alphabetically,
so they're easy to keep track of. Aaron? Introduce your
brothers and sisters to Kevin and don't forget baby Xavier."

She's got little pieces of fabric and paint samples.
She darts from room to room. "I'm thinking western
for you, Kevin. Cowboy curtains with a spread to match.
I can see an anvil and a real bale of hay right here by
your computer."

The living-room furniture is gone. Now there's
a big desk, a little desk, a globe, a blackboard—
and a whip. "Homeschooling is best," she says.
"Seven hours a day should do it. And sports
are just a distraction. So no more baseball."

She glides in as soon as the sun goes down.
"For God's sake," she cries, "cover those mirrors!
Hmmm. Such an alabaster neck for a boy.
Come give your new mama a kiss."

She's dressed in green scrubs, but they're torn
in two places. "Did your dad tell you I work
in a ward for the criminally insane? Well,
sometimes I have to bring my work home.
I'm so glad there are twin beds in your room."

"I'm an underwear model, Kevin. I'm sure you
and your friends have seen me in catalogs.
I'll come by school to pick you up in my
Who-Knows-When-It'll-Catch-on-Fire bra."

Trash

We almost lost to Papa's Pizzeria. We stranded more
runners than I want to remember. Everybody had
an iron glove: balls bounced every which way.
Did I help? No way. I got the big O-fer.

I call Mira on the way home. Balm for my wounds.
Those soothing vowels of hers. Instead she wants
to know if I'm aware that there are only about one
hundred and forty whooping cranes left in the wild.

"And they mate for life, Kevin. Isn't that sweet?"

Unlike my dad, who all of a sudden wants to
date for life.

And then I come around a corner and see them:
boxes full of Mom's stuff in the driveway—the coat
she wore to speed-walk in, the dressmaker's dummy
she used when she sewed (it's headfirst in a garbage can),
magazines she'd saved, and shoes. Mom loved shoes.
And they're all over the place like they fell from the sky.

I meet my dad on the porch. He's got another armful
of the past.

"Oh, jeez," he says. "It's you. I was gonna load this stuff up. . . . I didn't think you'd be home so soon. . . . I didn't want you to see this. . . . I just didn't want to look at her things every day anymore. . . . I'm tired of being sad all the time. . . . I'm sorry . . . I'm just . . . Are you okay?

I push past him and climb the stairs three at a time.

How Could You Do That?

Little by little
you gave everything away.
I couldn't believe it.

I couldn't believe it.
You just threw her away.
You think you're so smart.

You think you're so smart.
I know life goes on. I know.
Just stop saying it.

Stop saying it.
Let's talk about something else.
Let's talk about shoes.

Yeah, let's talk about those.
Her favorite shoes.
The ones you just threw away.

How could you do that?

On the Way to Anna's

Dad and I avoid each other. Even in the car
we're far apart.

He's probably thinking about Anna.
I'm thinking about "How Could You
Do That?"

I take refuge in poetry. I wonder what
he does.

I'm glad I've got this diary, because I
was really mad and I might have said stuff
I was sorry for.

That poem's got some pantoum in it
and maybe a little villanelle, but it's mostly
something I made up.

I like how the last line of every stanza
came right back at the top of the next one.

That's what I felt like doing—saying it.
And then saying it again.
Hitting him with it.

All of a Sudden He Blurts

"Kevin, I'm sorry about yesterday
when you saw Mom's stuff in the drive—"

I tell him, "I'm sorry I saw it, too."

"I could have used better judgment; the timing
wasn't exactly perfect."

"You can say that again."

"Are you too mad to go to Anna's? I'll take
you home if you want me to."

"No, I'll be all right."

"You're sure?"

"Don't worry. I'm not going to ruin dinner
with your girlfriend."

Anna's Place I

From the outside her condo looks like all the other condos.
But Dad knows his way. It's weird to think he's been
here before.

The door to 1116 is open, but we knock anyway.
Somebody says, "Come in!" Her voice reminds me
of Mira's: imported.

Whoa! China cows, wooden cows, a black-and-white
throw for the sofa, a cow candy dish. Cow salt-
and-pepper shakers. Not one bull.

I look at Dad. "I should have worn my anti-whimsy
hat."

"Lighten up," he warns me.

Hello, hello. Nice to meet you, nice to meet you.
She's pretty. Incredible, night-colored hair.

I think about ways to describe it. *Sable* sounds
like a compliment; *inky,* so-so; *sooty,* not so good.

So do the words I use decide how I'll feel about her?

Anna's Place II

Fish and rice for dinner, then something
called *Halo-halo*. She's impressed
that I'm the only kid. Anna has ten thousand
relatives.

Not really. But there's a lot and she sends
money back every month. Is that why
she's interested in my dad?

After dinner, some TV and Anna falls asleep.
"One fourteen-hour day after another," he says.
We rise from the couch, quiet as mist,
and drift into the kitchen. When Mom was sick,
we did a thousand dishes together.

I wash, he dries and puts things away.
I wring out the yellow sponge one last time
and say, "That was fun. Maybe we can
vacuum next time."

"It happens a lot. She works really hard.
Wait for me in the car, okay? I want to
say good night."

Oh, my God. They're going to make out.

Sunscreen, Sturdy Shoes, Hat,
Old Clothes, Gloves

I meet Mira by the Arroyo Seco Bridge. We lock our bikes
to the same tree and get in the back of a big orange pickup
with some other people.

A guy with a thick ponytail tells us about the river:
fifty-one miles long, a source of water for the Gabrielino
Indians a long time ago, 37,000 tons of trash hauled
out last year. We're helping make it beautiful again.

He's eating a burrito wrapped in tinfoil and he waves it
around like a baton. I wonder if Amy could play the piano
if he was conducting the *Carne Asada Suite for Steinway
and Appetite.*

"What are you thinking about?" Mira asks.
I answer. "You."

Our driver knows the way right down to the river's banks.
Which are concrete. Like the bottom. Which is hard to see
for the crud: grocery carts, plastic bottles, Styrofoam cups.
A guy right beside me says, "We found a cow last year."

We're watched by giant cats. Huge storm-drain covers,
actually, that taggers added giant whiskers to. And
big eyes, the better to see us with.

Somebody squawks into a megaphone, and a bunch
of ducks lift off: a new predator, for all they know.

There's a kind of log that's made an impromptu dam,
so another guy and I each take an end and carry it
away. The sick river gargles, then spits.

Some noir-types with a lot of peroxide and suede
shoes sit in a bathtub and take phone-pictures
of each other. They tell everybody they're looking
for the exact sites of the Blink-182 and Korn videos.

Mira marches over and lectures them, so they
take pictures of her and laugh. She wants everybody
to be serious like her.

After a few hours, the water doesn't look so dazed.
Somebody bikes past and offers me a granola bar.
An orchid corsage floats right by me and then
a paper boat on its side. There's something
about those two things together . . .
I decide to take a break and write in my secret diary.

Mira looms over me. When I look up, her head
makes a solar eclipse.

Her: "What are you doing?"

Me: "Don't worry. I'm not growing cotton or torturing an endangered specie."

She flounces away. Now I can't connect that orchid and the paper boat. I half-remember some story: in China a long time ago eunuchs would float poems out of the palace on red leaves. But it's gone now. Poems are super-sensitive. I won't get a second chance with this one.

I'm trudging back to work when I see somebody else hunched over a notebook. It looks like . . . No, it can't be.

"Hey, Shakespeare!"

It is! "Amy. What are you doing here?"

"We come every year." She points at random. "My mom's here somewhere."

"What are you writing?"

"Bad poetry. Want to see?"

Concrete. Mosquitoes.
All kinds of crap everywhere.
Me with a headache.

I tell her, "If you took out the first period in the first
line, it'd be more fun to read."

She takes the notebook back, frowns, then grins.
"Concrete mosquitoes. Cool." She pats
the cement and I sit beside her. She's warm
and radiates. She smells like mango.

"What if I e-mailed you some stuff and you told
me what was wrong?"

I shake my head. "You weren't wrong."

"Okay, I was predictable. That's worse than
being wrong."

"I don't know that much about poetry, not really."

"You know more than I do, buster. It'd be a secret,
too. Nobody has to know, especially not your
girlfriend."

"How do you know about Mira?"

"I asked around. Didn't you ask around about me?"

"That's a trick question, isn't it?"

"Give me your e-mail address. I'll send you some
stuff tonight. I was working on this sonnet
when the Muse came to the door with a cheesecake
and told me I could have it if I stopped."

"That's never good."

"So tonight, okay? And now return to yon goodly
creatures. 'How beauteous mankind is.'" She holds out
one hand and I help her up. "*The Tempest,*" she says.
"In case you were curious."

I'm pushing a grocery cart full of stuff that looks
like it came from the River Styx and not the River L.A.
when Mira heads me off.

"Who was that?"

"Who was what?"

"Who was that girl in the shorts?"

"Oh, just somebody I know from a poetry reading."

"Why couldn't she get up by herself?"

"She was pale and wan."

"She's pretty."

"If I say, 'Yeah,' then you're mad. If I say, 'No, she's not,' you'll think I'm blind."

Mira looks at the ground. "I'm insecure."

"Don't be. She's just somebody I met once. We talked about debris."

"Write me a poem."

"Now?"

"Whenever. But do it, okay? It doesn't have to be about me, just *for* me, okay?"

Then she kisses me with a lot of enthusiasm.

River Haiku

Even with big boots
somebody steps on a nail—
one less volunteer

Everything Mira
has on is relentlessly
green polyester

A homeless guy picks
up a ruined dollhouse and
stares in the window

There's not much current
but the tiny frog has to
fight hard anyway

Three feral cats wait
like goalies for the rats to
try and get past them

A Haiku Just for Mira Because She Asked

Five a.m. It won't
be long now and day will lay
out its merchandise

Toxic Haiku Fallout

Me	Her
Hey, Mira. What's up?	You sent me a poem.
Yeah, I wrote a lot of them down by the river so I wrote one for you, too.	So it's for me?
Sure.	It doesn't have my name in it.
I know, but it's still just for you.	It's short.
It's a haiku.	I thought those had to have frogs in them.
Not American haiku.	Does it mean anything?
Just what it says.	Is it about death?
No, it's about this morning. I couldn't sleep, so I looked out the window.	Are you sure it isn't about death? Teachers always say poems are about death.

That's just nuts.
Mr. B. doesn't say that.

Oh, who cares about Mr. B. I wanted a nice poem, and this one is about shopping. You can't say *merchandise* in a poem.

I can say anything I want.

I can't show this to Jennifer. Can't you write something with *moonlight* in it?

I'm not a vending machine.

Sometimes you are so impossible!

Things I Heard on the Way to Class

1. So I go, like—you know. And he goes . . . God!

2. He breathes funny.

3. The last piece of pie, I swear to god.

4. The phone goes all the way in your ear, right to your brain almost, but you talk into your thumb, I think.

5. He sits behind me—that's how I know.

6. Don't ask. It was my mother's idea.

7. It's a souvenir. From yesterday.

8. If Norman kissed me, I'd die.

9. Mojave Dan. No way am I calling my dad Mojave Dan.

10. Stilts. He came over to my house on stilts.

11. But what if your mother calls my mother?

12. I'm not going to copy. Just let me see what you wrote.

Now What? I

I wonder if any of those things I just heard will turn into
a poem someday. The one about stilts, maybe? Or the dad
who wants his kid to call him Mojave Dan?

I make notes almost every day, but today for sure because
I don't want to think about Mira. She's mad about that haiku.

She might stay mad until I write about moonlight. My mom
was like that: she'd go tight-lipped and just seethe. Dad
and I got quiet as smoke.

It's funny. Right after she died, I only thought good things
about her.

Now What? II

The signs aren't good. Four girls just came out
of the bathroom. Three of them are holding up
the fourth one who's sobbing and blowing her nose.
They're patting her and trying to make her eat corn
chips. She's like the llama at the petting zoo.
The llama of love. Because she's crying about
her (former) boyfriend. "He was at the movies
with Becca! Everybody saw them!"

That's pretty much how it's done. Almost nobody
says, "We're breaking up." Let technology do it.
Subject: Termination. Or a text message: I NEED
SUM SPACE. Man, that's cold.

Some guys go postal when they get dumped and start
following the girl everywhere. Outside her classroom,
behind her at lunch, a hundred e-mails a day.

Observation—guys like that never play sports.

Fabian has always had girlfriends. And somebody
he was with two months ago comes around again
sometimes, like the purple car on the Ferris wheel.

I've seen three of them watch him play center field:
former girlfriend, present, and future.

I turn a corner and there's Mira. The two girls she's with see me first and disappear. Like they went right up to the mother ship.

Mira runs up, puts her arms around me, and says, "I'm sorry. My parents are arguing a lot. I'm all confused. I read that haiku again, and I like it now."

Man, you just never know, do you?

Charm Colors

It's just the name of a team we play,
but I can't take them seriously. *Charm*.
What's that got to do with baseball?

What a charming double play. What
a charming bat. I love your cleats, they're
charming.

Daisy's Diaper Service wants to sponsor
a team, but nobody'll take them up on it.
Big surprise.

So we are merciless with Charm Colors.
We own those guys. We squeeze-bunt
with the bases loaded and their charming
catcher falls down going for the ball.

Mira comes to the game (for a change)
and afterward strolls down and hangs
over the little fence. She takes off my
first baseman's mitt and wears it. She
puts my hat on backward. She whispers
things in Spanish I can't understand, then
blushes.

Just then Morton Gluck goes by, sniping
at the littlest guy on the Charm Colors team.
That's bad enough. Then he brays,
"And where's that skank you call your
girlfriend?"

It's not about Mira, but I tell him, anyway—
"Watch your mouth, Morton."

"You're next, smart guy. It's just going
to be you and me."

"Whenever."

It's not that I'm not a little scared.
I'm that, all right. But what am I supposed
to do? The guy's a creep.

"If you fight him," says Mira, "I will never
speak to you again."

I've Got Mail!

To: Shakespeare
From: A total beginner
Subject: Partners in Poetry

Remember me? Amy from the river?
I know I said I'd send something immediately,
but I got busy.

So let's start now, okay? How about some haiku?
Baby steps.

I sat down in Book Bungalow's poetry section
and read a bunch of haiku from Basho
and Issa and some other guys.

A few too many leaves for me. Made me want to
get out my rake. In the moonlight. While it snows.
On my pet frog.

So here's an American haiku:

> Phone call from my dad.
> Honky-tonk music again.
> Of course he loves us.

Now you send me one, okay?

Small Problem

She doesn't have a nickname like Shakespeare. So is it
Dear Amy
Hi, Amy
Hey, Amy
Dear A?

Dear A sounds like I'm writing to my report card. "Dear A,
so nice to see you again. Don't be a stranger."

Hey, Amy sounds like I'm yelling at her.

Hi, Amy is okay. Casual. Offhand. Unpremeditated.
Neutral valence.

Howdy, Amy. No way. Not unless I suddenly inherit
a horse.

Dear Amy is fine. Everybody starts letters like that.
E-letters, too.

Amy all by itself is too stern.

Okay, then it's *Dear Amy.* Or I could just put *Nice Haiku*
in the subject line and that'd be that.

To: Ms. Beginner
From: Kevin
Subject: Nice Haiku!

Just mysterious enough but not baffling.
Sometimes I read poems and I don't get them.

I might not totally get yours, but it's not like
it could mean anything anybody wants it to.

I hate it when people say that. A poet works
a long time on something. Then some bozo reads
it and says, "Boy, that sure reminds me of the time
I detached my retina."

Like in yours — the Dad character calls
from a bar or club or concert and automatically
says what he always says.

The story is really compact and maybe
a little elusive, but not murky.

Here's mine —

                    Five a.m. It won't
                    be long now and day will lay
                    out its merchandise

Self-Interrogation

Me #1: Now are you proud of yourself, Kevin?

Me #2: What? All I did was send her a haiku.

Me #1: You sent her Mira's haiku.

Me #2: It was handy.

Me #1: Oh, please. You want to see if Amy gets it. It's a test.

Me #2: It's not a test. It's —

Me #1: Admit it. You just want somebody to like your poem.

Me #2: Why is that bad? Everybody wants somebody to like the stuff they do.

Me #1: You could have written another haiku. They're only seventeen syllables.

Me #2: It's a second opinion, okay? Like seeing another doctor.

Me #1: You're just mad at Mira. You want her to be wrong.

Me #2: She's already wrong.

Me #1: See? You're mad.

Me #2: Fine. I'm mad. Now are you happy?

To: Mr. Insight
From: Amy
Subject: Good eye, Sherlock

You, my friend, were right on the money
with my haiku: Dad's a musician (guitar and
mandolin). He tours a lot more than he's home.

And he makes these duty-calls after the gig
and he makes them to the bookstore phone
downstairs so—he claims—he won't wake
anybody up

but really it's just his way of not having
to talk to Mom or me as if we'd have
the effrontery (Nice word, huh?) to ask him
when he's coming
home.

So he just reads off the index card
he undoubtedly carries that says
SAY "I LOVE YOU" BEFORE
YOU HANG UP.

He's not a bad guy, but Mom and I have
totally got his number.

What's next: Pantoum? Sestina? Epic
poem in the manner of the *Aeneid*? That
should only take about three years.

Maybe we should do what everybody
says and write about what we know.

So—what's your school like?

To: Amy
From: Kevin
Subject: "T'was the Night Before Geography"

Meet picky Ms. Baldwin, she acts like a czar.
And she doesn't like near, but she's hot for afar.
She's got maps in her briefcase and maps on her clothes.
And I'll bet she can even draw maps with her toes.

Color Africa red, color India blue.
(All those poor, jaundiced farmers in yellow Peru.)
She's obsessed with the Nile, both the Blue and the White,
and those islands that only appear by moonlight.

A tour of the wetlands, the great dripless Gobi,
a Swiss canton or two, a bitter Nairobi.
That's okay—it's just stuff from the books on the shelf.
What's a drag are the times she starts in on herself.

So she's gabbed with yaks and a vicious vicuña,
faced down fiery red ants and rampaging tuna.
So she's seen the good gnus from a hot-air balloon,
played a round of croquet with a blue-faced baboon.

The way she can go on with these stories from hell
makes detention look good. I can't wait for the bell.

To: My partner in crime (poetry variety only)
From: Your local Chopin
Subject: "All Alone by the Metronome"

Of course you know the metronome.
(I hope there's not one in your home.)

In music class, it's tick, tock, tick.
It's just enough to make me sick.

I hate to see my teacher start
that steady ticking like a heart

that beats 4/4 both night and day
while music majors' brains decay.

No wonder when that class gets out
I like to run around and shout

and stumble when I try to walk
and mumble when I try to talk.

I've had it with the steady life.
I'm ready for a little strife!

Back and Forth as Fast as We Can

Me: Nice! The meter is perfect. A poem
about a metronome should sound like
a metronome, and this one really does.

Her: What about the word *strife*? I'm not sure
I mean strife. But it rhymed with *life*.

Me: Yeah, that's the weakest couplet.

Her: Dang it. I wanted to send it out.

Me: To a magazine?

Her: An online one, yeah. Don't you want to
be published?

Me: I don't know. Sure, I guess.

Her: Never too young to be famous, Shakespeare.
I gotta go. TTYL. Oh, I'm trying the sestina
next. How about you?

I Have to Hand It to Her

The sestina is almost impossible. I tried one once
and after a couple of stanzas threw myself onto
the nearest chaise and wept. Copiously.

Not really. But poets like Percy Shelley did
stuff like that. They were sooo sensitive.
Percy was always pretending to be a dead leaf
or chatting with the west wind.

I didn't give up on the sestina because
I was too sensitive. It was just too hard
for me. I was outclassed.

Fabian, Greg, and I were playing pickup ball
with three high-school kids once, and it was just
one frozen rope after another. We needed
the kind of helmets soldiers in Iraq wear.
We needed flak jackets.

The sestina was to me as those guys were
to us.

It's a cool form, I have to admit. No rhyme,
no meter, lines as long as you want, six lines
per stanza, six stanzas.

BUT the last words of those six lines
are the only words you can use to end
every line in the next six stanzas!
AND in a different order every time!

And if that isn't bad enough, you have to
use the six key words in the last stanza
BUT it can only be three lines long!

I like Amy already. If she can write
a sestina, I'm gonna love her madly.

Admire her, I mean. I'll admire her
madly.

Palettes of Plates

I listen to a crisp single and look up.
We're not taking these guys seriously.
They're usually as fragile as their
sponsors: guys on the DL, weak
dribblers to the mound.

"You know Becca Livermore?" Greg
asks. "She kept riding her scooter
back and forth in front of my house
last night. She's hot, but do I really
want my name written on her tummy
like everybody else's?"

Our turn to bat. Warren first, then
Brewster. They're miserable hitters,
and everybody knows it. Their
dads make them suit up.

Greg whispers, "We're gonna
lose this one, and look who's waiting
to comfort me."

Leaning on the fence is Becca,
dressed like a consolation prize.

Warren and Brewster

They're good guys, but they can't
play baseball.

What they can do is math.
Brewster for sure. They sit
together at the end of the bench
and whisper about things like
perpendicular bisectors and
quadratic functions.

Warren usually wears his glove
on his head. That drives Coach
crazy but he has to put them in
sometimes because their parents
are in the stands.

Brewster's dad drives for UPS
and shows up at the game in
his brown shirt and shorts. His
legs are thick as hydrants.

Brewster is wispy. If his dad
is a moose, he's a fawn. An oak
and a lilac, a semi and a Prius,
rock and paper.

To: Kevin
From: Brave enough to try a sestina
Subject: "Frankenstein's Assistant Gets a Letter"

It's about your son, little Igor.
He isn't the student we hoped.
He doesn't play well with his peers.
He always eats lunch alone.
We don't think it's only the hump.
How are things at home?

He doesn't seem to feel at home
here at Swansdown. He's the only Igor,
for one thing. Then there's the hump.
We thought he'd made friends with Hope,
a girl with fangs who also eats alone.
We thought perhaps they were peers.

Once or twice they managed to peer
at each other. But then she sprinted home.
So that was that. Once again, he's alone.
We're really at our wits' end with Igor.
Time after time we've had our hopes
crushed by, we fear, that hump.

We hate to keep bringing up the hump
but it's such a distraction for his peers.
And then there's the traumatized Hope.
The last we heard, she's still at home.
He really is such an Igor.
We've never seen someone so alone.

On the plus side, he seems content alone
with—how shall we put it—his hump.
God bless him. He's just who he is—Igor.
If even two of his Swansdown peers
could find their inner Igors, he'd be home
free. So there's always hope.

Really this letter is full of hope.
We don't want your son to be alone.
We certainly don't want to send him home.
Have you seen a doctor about that hump?
We long to see him happy with his peers.
Call us. Let's talk about Igor.

Please don't give up hope at your home.
Igor isn't doomed to be alone.
Someday some peer is bound to like his hump!

High Fives for the Sestina Queen

Me: That was wicked good. You even got the last stanza.

Her: The tercet, yeah. But all I did was look up the pattern for the words on the end and follow along. It was like paint-by-numbers.

Me: No way. Anybody can do paint-by-numbers. Poets crash and burn trying sestinas all the time.

Her: It seemed like the right word just kept coming around at the right time.

Me: Except they don't just circle, they trade places!

Her: I was probably just lucky.

Me: Well, you were lucky twice, because Igor is a great subject.

Her: I'll bet you could write a sestina if you wanted to.

Me: I'll bet I couldn't. Anyway, you're like the guy batting 1000 against southpaws. You own the sestina. I'll do something else, though. Couplets, maybe.

Her: Fast, okay? I'm not big on delayed gratification.

To: Amy
From: Kevin the Impaler
Subject: "Dracula Tells All"

I swear to god, I like the flying best.
The sun goes down, it's dark there in the west.
At last I rise intact from that pine box.
Then all I have to do is change my socks.
I'm ready for some fun up in the sky
before I have to land and terrify
some tourist in a flimsy negligee
who's come to Plasma Heights on holiday.
A maiden is my favorite midnight snack,
the goal of my crepuscular attack.
She's mine until some wise guy with a stake
decides to give this count a real heartache.
That's why I like a life more on the wing.
I feel so free up there. I almost sing
as I do barrel rolls and loops and dives.
No fretting over dozens of pale wives.
Alas, my freedom only lasts a while,
and then I have to find that creepy smile
and turn into Count Dracula again,
a man who lives his life, alas, in vein.

To: Kevin
From: Amy
Subject: Monsters R Us

Her: I <u>love</u> Dracula changing his socks!

Me: Thanks, but couplets aren't as hard as sestinas.

Her: Except when they are. I tried 'em and they just stunk
     up the place. Bah-dum, bah-dum, bah-dum, bah-dumb,
     bah-dumb. Clunk!

Me: Did you stop at the end of every couplet?

Her: Aren't you supposed to?

Me: Probably not all the time. Too many clunks.

Her: See, that's why I need you. To tell me stuff. I read
     about couplets but I didn't read that.

Me: So what's next?

Her: More poetry! If we do fifteen or so about monsters,
     we can enter a chapbook contest. Get our names
     on the cover. *The Dracula Files,* right? By
     Kevin Boland and Amy Gwynn. All monsters
     all the time! Get to work, lazybones.

I Have to Break Up with Mira

It's the only honest thing to do. People break up
all the time. It's not fair Verona where this scene
is laid. It's middle school. Nobody's going to
drop by any tombs at midnight with deadly potions.

I'll just explain things to her. She'll understand.
I'll say that I've got this new poetry-friend and . . .

No, wait. I'll say that I met this girl at a poetry
reading and we have a lot in common, so . . .

And we don't?

I can hear that one now. I sure don't want her
to start crying by her locker.

If Amy was cuter, I could just say that.
Be really callous and superficial.

Except Amy's not cuter. She's a whole lot more
fun, though.

How shallow is that? "I don't want to see you
anymore because you're not fun."

Except Mira and I did have fun. Sometimes.
Just not poetry fun.

All I really have to say is that I like somebody
else better. Short and sweet. Right to the point:

I like somebody else better.

Five words. I can handle that.

Dressed to Kill

I can't figure out what to wear
when I break up with Mira.

Somehow it seems to matter.
My black suit is a little obvious.
But I don't want some stupid T-shirt
with SLAYER on it, either.

Jeans or khakis? Short sleeves
or long? And shoes—I've got some
green high-tops that seem all wrong.
But sneaks seem right. I might need
to get out of there in a hurry.

Maybe I should look homeless.
Show up with a grocery cart
and a dog-on-a-rope. Then she'll
be glad to see me go.

I settle on jeans and a purple T
(Mom used to say purple was
a healing color).

Here she comes with Jennifer, who's
(Oh, man) crying. When they
get to me, Jen leans on Mira.
Her whole body is shaking.

I ask, "What happened?"
Mira snarls, "Lenny Boggs
just broke up with her and
do you know why? Do you

know what he said? 'I like
somebody else better.' Can
you believe that? Why didn't
he just stab her right in the heart?"

Dinnertime

We're just sitting down when a big moth
comes out of nowhere and flutters around
the mini-chandelier. Dad gets the same
little plastic cup and postcard that Mom
used, traps the moth, and carries him outside.

"Anna hates bugs," he says, picking up
his fork.

"Yeah?"

"She shakes her shoes out every time
she puts them on. She grew up really
different from anybody I ever knew.
Dirt floor, outdoor plumbing."

He wants me to like her a little.

How hard would that be?

The Dark at the Top of the Stairs

Dad and I do the dishes. Then I go up
to my room and read Amy's sestina again.

Wow! I wonder if we really could get
enough poems together to make a little
book like *The Dracula Files*.

When the phone rings, I'm pretty sure
it's Mira. She's been bugging me to
write her another poem.

Kevin, I just called to say that Jennifer
is never going to like another boy as long
as she lives. She's going to live in a
nunnery on top of a snow-covered mountain.
I'm her best friend, so I'm going too.

Mira: Kevin? Hello, Kevin?
Me: Huh? What?

It's for the best. Don't try and stop me.
You'll meet somebody new. In fact,
do you remember that girl in the blue
shorts you were talking to at the river?

She seemed perfect for you. I'll talk to
her before Jennifer and I take our vows.
She'll help you forget me.

Mira: Kevin, are you there?
Me: Huh?
Mira: What's wrong with you tonight?

So this is good-bye forever, dearest.
Jen and I are better off in a little cold
room with just a Bible and a lizard.
And you're better off with a girl who's
interested in your poems, which, I have
to say, I never really was. Or baseball,
either.

Mira: Well, I'm hanging up. This is
the stupidest conversation I've ever had!

To: You
From: Me
Subject: "Transylvanian Limericks"

A funny old guy is Count Drac.
He tries to look cool in all black.
Did he never think
to try something in pink
with a row of pearl buttons in back?

I thought I had met my dreamboat:
the accent, those eyes, that swell coat.
But when we eat out,
he never has trout.
He always goes straight for my throat!

I leave my door open at night,
turn the mirror to the wall, cut the light.
But then he comes in,
with type A on his chin,
and I tell him to go fly a kite.

He said he'd buy me a house,
the big, Romanian louse.
I end up in a crypt
with my good pants all ripped
and cobwebs all over my blouse.

To: Kevin
From: Amy
Subject: P.S.

In that fourth limerick, the I-leave-my-
door-open-at-night one? I wanted
the girl to be mad because Dracula
has been fooling around.

Did that work? Right before I gave up
I had
        But then he comes in
        with her type A on his chin
        so I tell him to go fly a kite.

but that second-to-last line stumbles.

But I'll fix it. Mom turned me onto
a book that says, "Writing is easy. Revision
is where the work gets done."

So I'll revise. Right now, let's crank out
some pages. Fame and fortune await us.

So Here's the Plan

I write a new Dracula poem (I've already
got the title: "The Undead."). I send it
to both Amy and Mira.

Amy loves it. It's clever, it's poignant, it's cute . . .
whatever.

Mira hates it. It doesn't have her name in it.
It's not about love. Poems can't be about
vampires . . . whatever.

Amy decides she wants to be more than poetry
pals. We plan to see a lot more of each other.

Mira's not sure about us anymore. I don't
use recycled paper. I don't separate
cardboard and cans.

We're not compatible after all.

Perfect.

The Undead

In those movies, there's always
a leading lady who isn't afraid
of anything. "You all go on to
the Garlic Festival," she says.
"I'll be fine here alone. In my
nightgown. With the window
open."

The count only bites her a little
at first. Then she's just drowsy,
but he comes back for more
and the local professor starts
sharpening his wooden stakes.

You know what happens next:
the crypt, the sunlight, The End.
People shudder and put on their
coats and hats.

Then everybody walks home
a little faster — down the dark
streets, past the white houses
with the garlic over every
locked door.

These Arrive within Minutes of Each Other

To: Kevin, laziest poet in the world
From: Amy
Subject: "The Undead"

I thought we agreed
to use forms. This is free verse.
What a lazybones.

If I can answer
you in two haikus, you can
do the assignment!

A-

To: Kevin, best boyfriend in the world
From: Mira
Subject: "The Undead"

I love this poem! You're so clever
and smart! Thank you. Thank
you. Thank you!

XXXXXXXXXXXXX Mira

Let's Hear It for the Girl Who Likes My Poetry

I plan to meet Mira by the library.
It's a good place to be indiscreet.

Fifth-graders scream and run around like mad.
The boys have that gleam in their eyes.

The girls throw Slushees at the boys and shriek.
They call them names: Loser! Geek!

Translation: I Like You More Than I Can Say.
I like your haircut, your shoes, your jeans.

I find an out-of-the-way bench. I'm dreamy
and warm. I don't think about Amy.

I think about baseball—the sun off our blue
uniforms, just how much fun it is.

Guys I've known since T-ball. Guys who
aren't in hyper-drive all the time.

I'm not thinking of Amy.

Baseball is slow and green and pastoral.
The pace is definitely anti-caffeine.

Like the song says, "I don't care if I ever
get back." For a while, nothing can go wrong.

Then here comes Mira with the volume turned up:
she looks great, even better as she gets nearer.

She walks right over and sits on my lap.
The kids stare. We're who they want to be.

Mira kisses me, so I kiss her back.
Which helps me not think about Amy.

Everybody Should Have a Secret Diary

I love writing in here. I can talk to
myself and about myself at the same time.

That last poem was fun: it looks like
couplets but it's not. No meter to speak
of, just rhythm.

And I mostly buried the rhyme instead
of putting everything at the end.

I like it that sometimes the rhyme tells
me what I mean instead of me telling it.

Like just looking for something to chime
with *Mira,* I stumbled on *nearer.* Not
perfect, but the way I feel about her/us
isn't perfect.

I mean I'm making out with Mira
and thinking about Amy. That's
not exactly perfect!

What's Amy doing? I wonder.
And since when did she join
the Poetry Police?

The Playoffs: Game 1, Bottom of the Sixth

Brewster digs in. He taps the always-phantom
dirt out of his rubber spikes. The pitcher
winds up and throws some smoke.

I'm on first. Even from there I can see
Brewster close his eyes
and swing.

I'm off before he connects and, man, does
he connect. Their coach had brought
the outfielders in, so it's way over their heads.

Then the center fielder can't find the handle,
and we're all of us along the third-base line
waving Brewster home.

He doesn't even have to slide, but he does.
Badly. Really badly. So badly that he rolls
across the plate.

But he beats the throw. So it wasn't pretty.
It counts! And we win.

Jubilation in the Dirt

We've got the hero on our shoulders.
Coach Mitchell grins like he won
the lottery. Brewster's dad howls
like a wolf.

When we set him down on home plate,
the first thing Brewster does is find Fabian
and hug him.

Which reminds me of how close to being
little kids we still are.

"You pint-size little nobody.
You lucky little pygmy. You couldn't
do that again in a thousand years."

It's Morton Gluck. Leaning into the dugout
and ragging on Brewster. Who looks
at Fabian.

Who strolls toward Morton. Who starts
backpedaling. "I'll get you," he yells. "Some
dark night, man. You just don't know when."

My dad comes down from the top row
of the bleachers. "Are you going for pizza?"
he asks. "Do you need some money?"
I tell him Coach will take care of that.

"Who was that kid?" he asks. "The one
who seemed to be so upset."

"Just some jerk."

"Guess who called me about ten minutes ago?
Anna."

"What'd she want?"

"She says she misses me. I'll see you tonight."

Thinking of Anna reminds me to not think about
Amy. And to be glad Mira wasn't here to see
Fabian and Morton almost get into it.

She hates fighting. I guess she thinks
her precious polar bears do rock/paper/scissors
to see who gets the comfiest ice floe.

The Great Pretenders

I talk to Mira that night and tell her about
the game. She pretends to be interested.
Sometimes that makes me mad. How can
somebody, even a girl, not be interested
in the playoffs?

Except I pretend with Mira, too. When she tells
me to take short showers and save 6.9
gallons of water, I pretend to care.

The Dracula Duet

Amy e-mails me (at last!):
"Check out teenbard.com!"

So I do, and there are our poems,
her "Transylvanian Limericks"
and my "The Undead."

Her name and mine for all the world
to see. Together. Side by side.
Under the title *The Dracula Duet.*

I grab for the phone.

Me: I thought you didn't like that poem.
Her: Are you kidding?
Me: You called me a lazybones.
Her: Oh, don't pay any attention to me.
    There's a recital coming up
    and Chopin is making me nuts.
    "The Undead" is great. Teenbard
    wouldn't have taken it if it wasn't
    good.
Me: Do you know those guys?
Her: No way. It's just submit-online-
    then-wait-to-see-what-the-editors-
    say.

Me: They're so fast. My dad waits
     months when he sends out short
     stories.
Her: Maybe he should try middle-aged-
     bard.com?
Me: I'll tell him you said so.
Her: Write for both of us this week, okay?
     I'm useless until Friday. Gotta go!
     Fred's waiting.
Me: Who's Fred?
Her: Frederick Chopin. His girlfriend
     drove him crazy, so he wrote
     the Polonaise. Maybe we should
     have a love affair full of jealousy
     and torment, then I'd play better.
     I'll talk to you Saturday.

Jealousy and torment, huh? Sounds like
more fun than cleaning up the L.A. River.

I Check Out the Competition

Man, some of those poems on that teenbard site
are pretty good. Plus there's an interview
with some eleventh-grader who talks about
parataxis (which probably isn't the two yellow
cabs I think it is).

I don't get a few of the poems ("The hidden
sun cramps like a pomegranate") but I really
like the idea that there are all those kids
out there writing.

Kids from just past twelve to the last second
of nineteen. Kids like Amy and me. They
probably go to school and have little rendezvous
and play sports or flip burgers and sometimes
wish their parents would move to Alabama
and just mail their allowance on the first
of the month

but they write, too. Even if the Goths or the skate
punks make fun of them or call them names,
they sit down at the computer or take out their
notebooks and write poetry.

I like that a lot.

Amy's Recital or Fools Rush In

It's one of those almost-summer evenings
when the moon comes up a little before the sun
is down. "O impatient orb," the old poets
would say.

But I'm a new poet, so I'd say, "What are you
doing here so early? The party doesn't start
until nine!"

When I get there, people are streaming in.
A little kid is lying on the grass like a lower-
case *x*. There's a good crowd: Parents.
Friends. Fans. I wonder if I'm looking at
a pageant of geniuses.

I'm locking my bike beside a couple of others
when Ophelia comes up the walk from the parking
lot. "Kevin. Amy didn't say you were coming."

"She doesn't know. It's a surprise."

"Well, do you want to sit together?" she asks.

I open the door for her.

My mom would never have had a little gold pin
in her eyebrow. She would never have worn boots
the color of Cherry Coke. And green tights.
But it looks good on Ophelia.

"I hear you guys are writing a lot,"
she says.
"Pretty much. I'm better at that than I am at
baseball. We lost big time to Black & White
Cleaners today."
"Amy told me about *The Dracula Duet.*
Good for you guys." She points to a couple
of empty seats, then settles in.

A guy in a tie as loose as a noose gets up
and introduces himself as the principal!
"The program tells you who's who,"
he says, "so let's get started."

Cellos make a dark foresty sound
(or maybe it's just that sawing).

The violinist has a fresh Mohawk
but everything else (T-shirt, jeans,
sneaks) looks ancient.

Amy's in a cowboy hat, a black
western shirt with fringe.

She plays like a stampede.

I ask Ophelia, "Was that Chopin?"

"She gave up on Chopin two days ago.
That was Shostakovich. She's always
switching horses in midstream."

"She hasn't traded in poetry."

"Not yet."

Then the last student comes out.
Tall, killer smile, sure of himself.
I'm surprised the corners of the keyboard
don't turn up coyly.

He plays some serious stuff and it
sounds good to me. Then while everybody
is applauding, he bangs out about twelve
bars of rock 'n' roll and brings the house down.

He's the kind of guy who could eat beets
and tomorrow everybody would want beets.

"C'mon," says Ophelia. "Let's go get Amy."

Except it's not just Amy. It's Amy and him.
The pianist. Mr. Underlined and in Italics.
Student of the Evening, the Week, the Year
probably. And better-looking up close.

He's leaning into her. She's holding his hand.

I just stand there like a potted plant.

"Kevin! Cool!" She throws her arms
around me, then takes them right back.
"So what'd you think?"

You know how fish do that puckery-mouth
thing but words don't come out? I did that.

"Wait. Where are my manners? Mom, you
know Trevor. But Kevin doesn't." She looks
at him, then me. "Kevin's my poetry buddy,
aren't you, Kev?"

What Was I Thinking?

What was I thinking?
What was I thinking?
What was I thinking?
What was I thinking?
What was I thinking?
What was I thinking?
What was I thinking?
What was I thinking?
What was I thinking?
What was I thinking?
What was I thinking?
What was I thinking?
What was I thinking?
What was I thinking?
What was I thinking?
What was I thinking?
What was I thinking?
What was I thinking?
What was I thinking?
What was I thinking?
What was I thinking?
What was I thinking?
What was I thinking?
What was I thinking?
What was I thinking?

Conversations with Myself

Me #1: That's it for me and girls.

Me #2: What about Mira? If you thought
it was going to be hard to tell her
you liked somebody better —

Me #1: Don't remind me.

Me #2: — imagine breaking up with her
because you're through with girls.
Like she's going to believe that.

Me #1: She would if I became a hermit
and lived in a cave.

Me #2: Except you're a first baseman
who lives in a suburb. And anyway,
you like Mira.

Me #1: I liked Amy better.

Me #2: You didn't know Amy. Not really.
You were infatuated.

Me #1: I thought she liked me.

Me #2: She likes how you write. Trevor
probably does brain surgery in his
spare time.

Me #1: Let's not forget Mira's cute, and she's
a good kisser.

Me #2: She probably recycles those, too.

Me #1: My, my. Aren't we sensitive?

(A pause while my selves get a drink of water
and maybe split an energy bar)

Me #2: I was infatuated, wasn't I?

Me #1: Totally.

Me #2: There's nothing wrong with Mira.

Me #1: Are you kidding? She's hot.

Me #2: And I've got a girlfriend. Why can't Amy
have a boyfriend?

Me #1: Exactly.

Me #2: We can still work on poetry together.

Me #1: For sure.

Me #2: Unhampered by conflicting emotions.

Me #1: If you say so.

Me #2: And concentrate on baseball
and on winning the playoffs.

Me #1: There you go. High five!

Concentration Pays Off

I go four-for-four, drive in three runs,
dig low throws out of the dirt, and make
a circus catch in foul territory.

That helps put us two games away from
the championship!

Who needs girls when there's baseball!

I start to think maybe I could play
in the bigs after all. Someday:

standout in high school, full
ride to college, Arizona State maybe.

Top draft pick, fat signing bonus,
meteoric rise from AAA.

And no girls. Just baseball. I'll
live like a monk: chop my own wood
and meditate on the perfect game.

In the off-season I'll move to
a cabin in the woods and write.

But no girls. Maybe I'll get a dog,
and a truck. If I have to, I'll wear

a disguise if I want to go to a reading.
My dog can wear a disguise, too, if
necessary. A mustache, probably.

Publish real books, not just online.
Give them away after games
and sign autographs for every kid
no matter how long it takes.

If anybody asks me the secret
to my success, I'll tell them: hard
work, cold water, and no girls.

Jekyll & Hyde in the Suburbs

Dad says, "Anna's coming for dinner
Thursday night. Do you want to ask Mira?"

Fur sprouts all over me: I growl,
"Can we not talk about girls tonight?"

"Well, I was just thinking: Anna
and me, you and Mira, maybe Amy
and Ophelia from the bookstore.
Your mom and I used to have these
little dinner parties and—"

My fangs show: "First of all, Amy's a girl
and I really don't want to talk about girls.
Second, she's got a new boyfriend. And
third, I don't want to talk about Mom either."

"You okay, Kev? You seem a little,
I don't know, stressed maybe."

I throw back my head and howl.

"Maybe you'd be better off in your
room, kiddo. You're impossible tonight."

Advice from Jekyll to Hyde:
A Villanelle

Grow up, kid. It's not like you're in danger.
Anna's about as threatening as a fawn.
Stop treating her like she's a stranger.

It's not like she walked in with a derringer.
Look at that pretty skin—the color of cinnamon.
Grow up, kid. It's not like you're in danger.

Do you think she's some kind of rearranger?
She's not. Don't act like a simpleton.
Stop treating her like a stranger.

Do you really think she's an infringer?
No way. She's gentle and quiet as a swan.
Grow up, kid. It's not like you're in danger.

She's nice to you; be nice to her.
Stop acting even a little withdrawn.
Stop treating her like a stranger.

Dad just likes Anna. He doesn't worship her.
And what if he did? He's tired of being lovelorn.
Grow up, kid. It's not like you're in danger.
Stop treating her like a stranger.

Saved by the Villanelle

So Anna comes for dinner, and my evil twin
wants to take over.

I think it was just her walking around in
Mom's house that did it.

Everybody was nervous. I talked about
baseball. Then said good night.

She hugged me, which was cool. I went upstairs
and wrote that villanelle,

a form with more rules than San Quentin:
Only nineteen lines. Only two rhymes. Yikes!

It turned out okay, though. A little bit
of muscle here and there

to make the rhymes work, but not too much.
I could probably send it to teenbard.com

on my own. Who needs Amy, who's probably
busy slobbering all over Trevor, anyway?

We Win a Squeaker

Thanks to Pat Carrington, who's
good for about ten pitches.
But they're all strikes.

So he only plays when it really matters.
Like today. We're up 6–5 in the bottom
of the sixth and Blockbuster Video gets
men on.

So Patrick uncorks something out
of the dark netherworld of fastballs.
I'm surprised they don't smell like
sulfur and burn holes in the catcher's
mitt. Six of 'em in a row.

Then he collapses on the mound.

Which is pretty much what he always does.
And we run out and pick him up. His mom
is there with his inhaler.

We can't pound him on the back because
he's Patrick, so we kind of pet him like
a baby goat and tell him, "Good job, man."

Fans

I know Anna and Dad are in the bleachers.
A couple of rows down, Mira and the inevitable
Jennifer. Then I see Amy and Trevor!

He's pointing and telling Amy, probably,
how he stole home from first base once
blindfolded.

Dad introduces Anna to Mira and says,
"We'd take you two to eat if you want."

I point to the dugout. "I should, you know,
go with the guys probably. Show a little
team spirit."

Anna's got a nice good-bye smile. I see
Trevor and Amy making their way toward me.
Us. Mira and me.

Trevor's got a cool T-shirt with a horse
on it. His arms are bigger than mine.
He probably bench-presses his piano.

He holds out his fist, and I tap it.
"Nice game, man," he says.
I ask him if he plays. Ever played.

He shows me his hands. "My folks
made me stop."

Amy says, "Trevor played violin
with the San Gabriel Symphony when
he was six."

I say, "I could put my pants on by myself
when I was six."

Trevor laughs, showing more perfect
teeth than I've ever seen, then says,

"Let's get a Coke or something.
Hang out for a while, okay?" Amy
takes hold of my wrist and shakes
it. Shakes me. "Yeah, c'mon."

"Well, okay." I look toward the almost-
empty dugout. "Just let me tell the guys."

Mira looks at me like she can't believe it.

Mira's Like a Stick of Dynamite with a Long Fuse that Sizzles While the Four of Us Talk, but the Minute Amy and Trevor Split, She Explodes

"Unbelievable!"

"What?" I'm either playing dumb
or I really am dumb.

"You always go out with your boys
after a game. But all that Amy has
to say is one word: 'C'mon.'"

"Well, you were staring at Trevor
like you'd never seen a boy before,
so I thought—"

"So you did it for me? Then how
come all you and that Amy did was
talk about pantaloons?"

"Pantoums. And what do you care what
we talked about? You were busy
speaking Spanish with Señor Trevor."

She admits, "I just get jealous."

I reach for her hand. "Look,
you've got environmental
friends, okay? They're interested
in the same stuff that you are.
Amy and I are interested
in poetry; that's all there is to it."

There's one of those empty bus
places where you can wait out
of the rain. She leads me in there
and starts kissing me.

I don't imagine she's Amy.
I do wonder what that would be like.

I also wonder about what I just
told her. About Amy and me being
poetry friends.

It's true and it's not true. Or it's
true and I wish it wasn't. So it's
semi-true. Kind of.

So if I am semi-true with Mira,
is she semi-true with me?

To: My poetry pal
From: Smarty pants
Subject: Check this out!

Raven on Toast

Once upon a midday dreary, while I staggered weak and weary,
Through the lunchroom with its grungy, sticky, icky concrete floor,
What I saw there was so oddish, maybe prehistoric codfish?
Stewing camel wrapped in flannel? Tell me. Tell me. I implore.
Boiling cesspools of old toadstools. What pulsing, rotting, reeking gore.
Grossness here and nothing more.

Carefully my tray I carried, stacked at least with nothing hairy,
Brown Jell-O's just a little scary, nothing really to deplore.
While I sat and idly chattered, while the silverware just clattered,
In there walked a girl in tatters headed for the middle of the floor.
Her jeans were low, her top was cropped, showing what her tummy bore—
NORMAN PRATT: FOREVERMORE.

Deep into that navel peering, Norman stood there frozen, fearing.
There's his name where Rick's and Bob's and Zax's had been before.
And his eyes were weirdly gleaming like a cornered beast who's scheming.
But like some poor addled lemming, he just bolted for the door.
Shot right past her, as she stood there plastered to the lunchroom door.
Silence then and nothing more.

128

As she posed there looking pouty with her now defiant outie,
Girlfriends gathered round her crooning, "Norman's rotten to the core."
Someone volunteered her sweater. Becca scowled and quickly said her
Tummy wasn't cold. Her girlfriends sighed. They'd seen all this before.
Exit Becca, brokenhearted, telltale ink stains as her decor.
"Becca! Becca!" they implored.

His whole crew looked so chagrined. "Norman's really done it now.
He's just shy and all embarrassed. He didn't mean to get her sore."
Tell that to her girlfriends glaring, staring, plotting, and declaring
War on Norman for just leaving Becca at the lunchroom door.

All decked out in Magic Marker—that poor Rebecca Livermore.
Norm should head for Singapore.

Is this funny? Yes _____ No _____ Maybe _____

We Exchange Some Sharp Volleys (While I Don't Let on How Glad I Am to Hear from Her)

Me: Who's Norman Pratt?

Her: Nobody. A character in this story.
Don't tell me there's a real Norman
Pratt at your school. Is it funny?

Me: To me, yeah. To Becca, I don't know.

Her: It's not like she's going to see it. I don't
think she reads teenbard.com, do you?

Me: Why'd you use her real name?

Her: Because *Livermore* is such a great rhyme
with *nevermore*! I saw Becca prancing
around at the game and Trevor told me
about her. So when we were walking
home and he recited "The Raven,"
the whole parody just came to me.

Me: I sure know how that is. Right after you left,
Mira recited the *Iliad* in Spanish.

Her: Ha, ha. Trevor liked you guys. He said
you're a really good athlete. Do you
like him?

Me: How can you not like somebody who
spontaneously recites "The Raven"?

Her: Did I tell you he plays five instruments?

Me: All at once? I'd like to see that.

Her: Send me something new, okay? I miss
trading poems. I miss you. The recital's
over, so I'm back in the poetry business!

Me: We play for the championship pretty soon.
That's where my head is at right now.

Her: After that, then. After you win.

"I Miss You"

I think about what that means. Could mean.
I don't think too much, though. My head
really is in that championship game.

And the day starts funny. A rooster wakes
me up. Where did he come from? The sky
is all eyes-down like it's just been yelled at
unfairly.

And school to get through before the game:
semester projects, people in new pants they
hope will make a difference, Mira upset
about the family counseling sessions.

And what about that loudmouthed bully,
Morton Gluck? What if he wants to fight?

I see Greg and Fabian in the halls and we
don't say anything. We're saving every
ounce for four o'clock.

Dad drives me down to the ball field. Anna's
working. The last thing he says to me is a
quote from Jack Kerouac: "Rest and be kind,
you don't have to prove anything."

How cool is that? A lot of other dads have got
their kids by the shoulders, shaking them and
stoking the coals.

In the dugout, Greg points across the field.
"Check it out." Oh, man — it's Morton Gluck
on crutches. And the coach looks super-serious!

Everybody's standing around him, listening
and nodding. Morton's there and not there,
staring at the ground. On the DL. Totally
left out of everything.

I felt like that when I had mono, but I can't
see myself going over there and telling him.

It's a good game. Because we're really
evenly matched: 1–0, 2–3, 4–3, 5–5,
5–7, 7–8.

Their coach is amped. Nobody swings
at 3–0. His lineup order is good: the leadoff
man gets on every time. The hit-and-run
works phenomenally, and every time he
shifts the infielders, it's the right time.

Fabian stalks the dugout, reminding
everybody to bear down. I think about
what Kerouac said: "You don't have
to prove anything."

I always play hard. We all do. If we lose,
it's not because we're a bad team.

The coin flip let them bat second.
We're tied in the bottom of the sixth.

Coach puts in Pat Carrington, who's been
lying down the whole time, saving his
energy.

We don't even need his ten pitches
because there's two out. Men
on second and third, but two out.
Three strikes and we go to extra innings.

Everybody's on their feet. Pat's facing
a kid named Jaffe who's hitting about
.230. Jaffe is almost green with
responsibility.

0–1. 0–2. Their hats are on backward.
Parents are going nuts in the bleachers.
Then he connects. It's weak, a dribbler.
Fabian charges it. I'm leaning, glove way
out so it gets to first as soon as it can.

It takes a bad hop. Hits Fabian in the face.
I can see him wince, see the blood start.

Whoever's on third streaks home.

Game over.

Fabian straightens up, faces the stands
so his mom can see he's okay. Coach
trots out with a towel but Fabian shakes
him off.

He wants to bleed some more so everybody
knows it wasn't his fault. Not really.

That Night at Dinner

Dad and I tackle the crossword.
A five-letter word for this, a seven-letter
word for that.

We get *foiled* (the clue was *thwarted*)
and without looking up from the folded
newspaper, Dad says, "I'm sorry you guys
lost, but I'm glad it wasn't your fault."

"Me, too. I mean, I've done it and it really
sucks. But better Fabian than somebody
who doesn't play very often. Then he's
that guy forever. Everybody knows
Fabian's not that guy."

"Remember when I went to my high-school
reunion a couple of years ago? There were
jocks there still talking about who dropped
the ball in the big game."

"I'm hitting Fabian a hundred grounders
tomorrow. That's what we do
every time we screw up."

The Season's Over

I'm pretty much done with the kind of ball
we've been playing. High school is next.

I know the coach because he shows up
at games every now and then and checks

things out. Checks me out. What would he
think if he knew I liked poetry, too?

High-school ball scares me a little. Greg
and I ride our bikes over and watch.

Some of those guys are huge. The catcher
is built like a shed. One of the pitchers
has the meanest sidearm I've ever seen.
They spit like big-leaguers.

Some really good-looking girls sit
in the bleachers and watch.

Greg says, "You want to play
Resident Evil 5 tonight?"

I shake my head. "Can't. I'm going
to the movies with Mira."

Intrigue at the Multiplex

When her folks drop Mira off, I go up
to the car and say hi. I was reading poetry
the other day and there was this line I liked:
"buried in the dark of me."

That's what I think when I see Mira's dad,
who's always so stiff and formal. What's
buried in the dark of him?

I know he's in counseling with Mira's mom
and sometimes Mira, too. She doesn't want
to talk about it, but she hates it.

Tonight she seems okay. And she looks
great. A lot of guys check her out.

And then Jennifer shows up. Mira tells
me, "We're waiting for William." Then
Jennifer has to go to the bathroom. She's
always going to the bathroom. Jennifer
and her lentil-size bladder.

We wait by the concession stand, with its
little bleachers full of gummy bears,
M&M's, and Reese's Pieces.

I ask, "So are Jennifer and William going
together now?"

Mira shakes her head. "Not yet. But I told Ashley to tell Ella to tell Kaylee to tell Maya to tell Rick to tell William that Jennifer's going to be here tonight."

I ask, "How'd Rick get in there?"

"Rick's the guy who tells the guys. Maya can't tell William."

"I don't think I understand this."

"You don't have to. You've got a girlfriend."

I Wonder if Amy Has Seen This Movie

It's about this gorgeous girl who can't get a date,
so she gets fixed up with one troglodyte after
another.

Hilarity is supposed to ensue. My mind wanders:
I wonder if Amy is writing. Or is she too busy
making out with Trevor?

Mira nuzzles me, but that's just to show Jennifer
that she has a boyfriend and Jennifer doesn't.

The girl in the movie has a bee in her apartment,
so she has to call the good-looking neighbor.

I wonder if Amy and Trevor go on picnics.
If they do and if a bee shows up, I'll bet Trevor
would kill it.

I, on the other hand, would ask the insect
to leave, since I can speak Bee. And once
Amy heard that, she'd tell Trevor to get lost.

"Kevin, what are you thinking about?"

"Nothing."

To: Kevin
From: Amy
Subject: Is this good or just weird?

Blue Ghazal

I give up. I'm never going to sleep tonight.
Why do troubles always come out at night?

Is every kid at my school a #&*^@! genius?
I should pray to the Patron Saint of Night.

Why does everybody have allure but me?
I feel like I ought to only slither out at night.

My boyfriend's so cute, every girl envies me.
Try waiting for him to call every night!

I feel all puckered up, and not in a good way.
I type this out and submit it to the night.

How Cool Are You!

Her: Seriously?

Me: Are you kidding? Ghazals are hard! All those
     couplets that don't rhyme except for that one word
     you have to use over and over.

Her: A couple of lines are a little longer than the others.

Me: It's only a draft. Work on it some more.

Her: I showed it to Trevor and he didn't get it. He thought
     I just wanted him to call me earlier. That is so Trevor.

Me: Well, the second-to-last stanza is about him.

Her: Whose side are you on, anyway? Why didn't he love
     the last line like you did?

Me: Hey, give Trevor a break. He looks like the guy on
     an Abercrombie bag and probably plays "Amazing
     Grace" when he farts. (Or is that too crude?)

Her: Crude is gude/ Crood is good. Trevor is soooo
     refined.

Me: Feel free to e-mail me anytime at earthyhumor.org.

Her: I love writing to you. I always feel better afterward.

Me: Me too.

Her: Send me something, okay? Our monster collection
     is pretty skimpy. Over and out.

Me: Time to wait impatiently for Trevor's call?

Her: Dear Poetry Pal: Bite me!   xxooA

Boys Being Boys

Greg and Fabian and I go jogging after school.
I've known these guys forever, and we've always
been pretty much alike.

Now we're getting different. Fabian is
pulling ahead: a little taller. His voice seems
to get deeper and deeper. He's hairier.

Greg worries about his clothes more.
He likes to look sharp, and everything
has to be new. None of that vintage
stuff for him.

Girls like Greg, but they aspire to Fabian.
Me? I'm just Mira's boyfriend.

We go an easy three miles and talk while
we run. Cars at first. Will I drive my mom's,
the one she left when she died? A Buick.

I tell them, "I don't know. I used to think
no way, but maybe I'm changing my mind."

"Your dad's Jeep is cool," Fabian says.
Greg shakes his head. "The Buick is cooler."

"Some girls will go with a guy just because
he's got a sweet ride."

"Some guys will go with a girl just because
she's cute."

A couple more years till we're sixteen.
A year and a half for Fabian. Trevor's
almost sixteen now, I'll bet. He'll probably
get a Porsche for his birthday.

Just what he needs, right? Maybe
he'll be popular then.

To: Shakespeare
From: Neptune's daughter
Subject: Pass the Dramamine

Trevor's dad knows this guy who has a boat
docked somewhere around Malibu, so we all
drove down Sunday and went for a ride.

Way late in the season for whales, which is too
bad because if one came up and smashed into us
with his prodigious forehead and broke the boat
in half and then ate the crew, I could write
a monster poem.

I saw a porpoise, but what rhymes with that?
Sourpuss? Enormous wuss?
You see my problem.

Trevor was the only monster. The guy
who owned the boat brought his wife, who
was about two hundred years younger than
he is, and when Trevor was playing guitar,
she was maple syrup and he was a pancake.

But it's not his fault he's monstrously
gorgeous and talented. Maybe it just made
me remember what a mere mortal I am.

There's no poem there either. <u>And</u> I ate
too much lobster salad, so if a whale had
swum by, he'd have hit on me.

Later:

P.S. It'd be fun to see you at school, wouldn't it?
Pass each other poems in the hall. Leave them
in hollow trees to find on the way home. Mira
and Trevor would never have to know.

To: Neptune's daughter
From: Kevin
Subject: Secrets

Let's see if I've got this straight: you cast off
from Malibu on a yacht and eat lobster
salad while your boyfriend
serenades everybody.

You're right. It sounds horrible. I'm surprised
you held up under the strain.

But it would be cool to leave each other poems
in secret places. That sounds easier than me
telling Ashley to tell Ella to tell Kaylee to tell
Maya to tell Rick that I've got a sonnet for you.

The News at Night

Here's Amy's latest e-mail—

Sorry I'm so late writing today/tonight.
Trevor came over and we had pizza.
Lots of pizza and then some Mozart
piano duets plus some fun stuff
for four hands.

Unless a slimy tentacle comes out
of my closet in the next ten minutes,
I'm striking out on monster poems.

Fun stuff for four hands, huh?
I'll bet.

Just get used to it, Kevin.
Amy writes to you, but
she's with Trevor.

And Then Look What She Sent Me at Three A.M.

What I'd give for a giant lever.
Pull it and say farewell to Trevor.

I'd like to buy a great, big cleaver
and bury it in your forehead, Trevor.

I didn't think we'd last forever.
But fifteen days? You creepy Trevor.

I hope you get a giant fever
and waste into a mini-Trevor.

I didn't like you that much, Trevor:
barely a hemidemisemiquaver!

A Two-Word E-mail Question:
WHAT HAPPENED?

She doesn't answer while I'm in the shower.
She doesn't answer while I eat breakfast.

At school, I go to the computer lab twice to check
my messages. I borrow some guy's laptop
just before fifth period.

Nada, as Mira would say.

I decide to go home and if there's still nothing
by the time I get there, I'll call her and if she still
doesn't answer, I'll ride my bike over to the bookstore.

A Two-Word E-mail Answer: CALL ME I

When I dial, she picks up on the first ring:

Her: He dumped me.

Me: I figured. *Cleaver* was the tip-off.

Her: How stupid am I?

Me: I'm not touching that one.

Her: I go to lunch, okay? I get my tray,
     sit at Trevor's table like usual.
     All his friends fly away, you know?
     Like buzzards. Except I'm the road kill.

Me: So what'd he say?

Her: That he liked somebody better!

Me: Ouch.

Her: And guess who he likes better than me?
     Becca Livermore.

Me: Oh, man.

Her: Exactly. I thought he was different.
     I mean, you'd never want your name on
     Becca's disgusting stomach.

Me: I'm not sure she can spell *Kevin*.

Her: I knew he was a player. He's had like
     ninety-two girlfriends starting in
     preschool. So am I so shallow I just wanted
     to be seen prancing around with him?
     You and I can never like each other, okay?
     Promise me.

Me: But . . .

Her: I mean the way I liked Trevor and you like Mira.
I love you as a friend. I do. But I don't want
to like you and I don't want you to like me.
Look what happens! Promise me.

Me: Okay, I guess.

Her: We're just lucky you've got Mira, right?
Because now we can't like each other.
But we can be poetry friends forever.
We can be as serious as we want about
poetry, and it's not going to distract us
from our calling because that's poetry!
And remember that poem I wrote with
Becca's name in it, "The Raven" revisited?
I totally hate her and I am totally sending
it to that teenbard site!

CALL ME II

Her: Guess what! The old Orpheum in Glendale
is doing Monster Matinee this Saturday.

Me: Great. Let's go.

Her: Are you kidding? We can't do
that. It'd be a date.

Me: It wouldn't be a date. It'd be a field
trip. We're doing research.

Her: Cool! A field trip. Absolutely.
We won't hold hands, we won't
eat out of the same popcorn box,
we'll sit on opposite sides of
the theater.

Me: I think we'll be able to control
ourselves. We'll be busy taking
notes.

Her: Just kidding. We'll be fine.
And you'll tell Mira, anyway,
right?

There's No Way I'm Telling Mira

Nobody's going to see us in Glendale.
It's like three bus rides away.

I had to lie to Amy. What if I said
I wouldn't tell Mira and then Amy
said she wouldn't go unless I did?

I want to go to the movies with Amy.
I want to see all those monsters
and not hold hands.

Then I can write some more poems.
We can write some more poems.

But I can just see me telling Mira that
I'm going to the movies with this girl
she already doesn't like so that she
and I can write poems and publish
a little book together which might
mean a book tour to exotic cities
and crowded hotels with only one
available room.

Mira would probably beat me like a piñata.

Liar Liar Pants on Fire I

On Saturday I even lie to Dad because I just
don't want to get into it. He believes
me when I say I'm playing soccer
because I usually tell the truth.

So that means I have to wear soccer clothes.
Oh, man—now look. I'm wearing disguises!

So on the way home, am I going to have to
throw myself in the dirt to keep up appearances?

Mira's easier. She's picking up trash along
the freeway with some kids from church.
She'll take before/after pictures of the roadside
and send them to me.

Well, isn't that exciting? I can pore over those
before I go to bed.

Actually this field trip will be a good test.
If it's all about poetry, then that's that.
Which is fine. I love poetry.

And I still like Mira. A lot. Sometimes.

To: Kevin
From: Amy
Subject: I couldn't sleep so I wrote this

King Kong Loves Ann Darrow

They get away from those stupid little planes.
He's got her in his hand,
safe.

It's not easy (he's so tall) but they find a place.
Chairs she can sit in. A yard for him.

She shops and cooks. They eat on the patio
a lot.

He's not like the other guys. Big breaths
but he doesn't pant.

They're out in the country, so when it gets
dark and she goes outside in her pajamas,

she doesn't know if it's the lawn she's walking
on or him.

I Show Amy's Poem to an Expert

Dad reads it to himself. Sits down
and reads it out loud. Then he says,
"Wow."

"I know, now my girlfriend writes better
than I do."

He slips it in like an ice pick.
"Since when is Amy your girlfriend?"

"I didn't mean . . . I mean I meant . . ."

He scrutinizes me. "She's very different
from Mira, isn't she?"

"No kidding."

He looks down at the poem again.
"This is wonderful. The ape loves her madly;
she doesn't get it."

Wait a minute! Is this about Amy and me?
And if it is, who's the ape? And who loves
who madly? And who doesn't get it?

To: Shakespeare
From: A Talentless Nobody
Subject: A dagger to the heart

Her: Teenbard turned that Becca poem down flat!
They said if Becca Livermore is a real person
she could sue the site.

Me: Change the name.

Her: To what? Livermore is the perfect rhyme.

Me: How about Mabel Barrymore.
Or Lois Carnivore. Or Chubby Omnivore.

Her: Stop! I'm inconsolable. Aren't you
inconsolable for me?

Me: Sure, but I've seen my dad get so many
rejection slips, I guess I knew one was
coming sooner or later. We're fourteen
years old. We've got lots of time.

Her: Aren't you the voice of reason today?
Well, don't worry about me. I don't
know where the teenbard office is
and I haven't got a gun.   XXXXXA

News from the Front Lines

Mira's parents have declared war now,
so there's that. The worse it gets, the more
she recycles, worries about the wetlands
and the baby seals.

I think she wants to take care of the world
because her folks aren't taking care of her.

Amy and I have maybe eleven poems about
monsters now. She's been scanning the Net
for chapbook contests we can enter.

I call Mira. She talks about her parents
and she cries.

I call Amy. We talk about everything
and we laugh.

And Then

On Saturday Greg and Fabian and I are playing
soccer with some ninth-graders. They're pretty good
and that makes us play better.

Sports are great. I stop thinking and just play.
I get into it. Let the body take over.

Fabian stops me. "Isn't that Mira's mom's car?"

It sure is, and it's moving fast, and stopping fast
and the door flies open and Mira storms out
and comes right at me.

Greg holds up one hand and puts his foot on the ball.
Everybody watches me wait.

"Were you really at the movies with that girl?"

I nod. "Yeah."

Mira's got her fists clenched and I wonder if she's
going to hit me. "How could you!"

"We just went. For something we're writing.
It's not what you think."

(Except it is. It's exactly what she thinks.)

"Why didn't you tell me?" she demands.

"I don't know. Probably I thought you'd get mad. Like you are now."

"I'm mad because you cheated on me."

"Nothing happened. We didn't do anything except go to the movies."

Mira takes a step closer. Her eyes could scald me. "Do you want her or me?

"Look, Mira, why don't —"

"Her or me, Kevin! I mean it."

I'm starting to get mad. "I'm in the middle of this game, okay? So stop yelling."

Mira actually shakes her finger at me like we're in second grade. "Don't ever talk to me again, Kevin. Not ever."

She stalks away. Everybody watches her go. Fabian says, "Nice work, Romeo. Now can we play some soccer?"

Dad and I Eat Spaghetti

and read. He's got a book, I've got a book.
But I'm writing in mine:

I feel kind of bad about Mira. But I don't
want to talk about it.

He asks, "Do you remember Carla Keene?"

I shake my head. "Who's Carla Keene?"

"I ran into her in Pavilions today."

I put down my fork. "You picked somebody
up in the market?"

"I knew her. Your mom and I did. Carla's
divorced now."

"I was just getting used to Anna."

He nods. "I don't think I know what I'm doing."

"Hey, join the club."

WHY DIDN'T YOU TELL ME YOU GUYS BROKE UP !!!

Me: I was going to.

Her: Really? When?

Me: Christmas 2012, maybe.

Her: You're a funny guy. And I mean kind of odd.

Me: That's what I've been thinking lately.

Her: Were you worried I'd think we had to be
     totally together now?

Me: You said if we were boyfriend/girlfriend, we'd
     break up sometime, but if we were poetry
     friends, we could be that forever.

Her: But now we can hang out all the time.
     Write constantly and be the best poetry
     friends ever.

In the Bookstore Almost Every Day

I like it at Ophelia's Bungalow.
I feel at home. Sometimes I go upstairs,
where Amy is. Or if I don't, I read
and pet the cat, who curls up in my lap.
There's no TV, no Internet, no noise.
It's really fun to visit all these books —
a thousand stories at my fingertips.
When Amy's working on a piece for school,
some chords will trickle down. Then browsers pause
or sway a little by the sci-fi shelf.
Today she makes us tuna fish on rye.
She gives the cat a bite. She asks, "What's up?"
"Some more blank verse. I seem to love that stuff."
"I like to work upstairs when you're down here."
She sits. She kisses me. I kiss her back.
"We broke our rule," I say. "We aren't supposed —"
"Too late," she says. And kisses me again.

To: Amy
From: Kevin
Subject: "A.M. Tanka"

Are you awake yet?
The rain is getting fiercer.
Drop by drop by drop.
That's how I learned to like you.
First a little, then a lot.

P.S. Don't tell the guys I write stuff like this!

To Kevin
From: Amy
Subject: I totally love that tanka, and

I Won't Tell Anybody You Write Stuff Like That
Unless You Stop Writing Stuff Like That
to Me

XXXXXXXXXXXXXXXXXXXXXXXXXXXXXXXXX
XXXXXXXXXXXXXXXXXXXXXXXXXXXXXXXXX
XXXXXXXXXXXXXXXXXXXXXXXXXXXXXXXXX
XXXXXXXXXXXXXXXXXXXXXXXXXXXXXXXXX
XXXXXXXXXXXXXXXXXXXXXXXXXXXXXXXXX
XXXXXXXXXXXXXXXXXXXXXXXXXXXXXXXXX
XXXXXXXXXXXXXXXXXXXXXXXXXXXXXXXXX
XXXXXXXXXXXXXXXXXXXXXXXXXXXXXXXXX
XXXXXXXXXXXXXXXXXXXXXXXXXXXXXXXXX
XXXXXXXXXXXXXXXXXXXXXXXXXXXXXXXXX
XXXXXXXXXXXXXXXXXXXXXXXXXXXXXXXXO